Violet Mackerel's

Brilliant Plot

Violet
Mackerel's
Brilliant Plot

ANNA BRANFORD   SARAH DAVIS

WALKER BOOKS
AND SUBSIDIARIES

LONDON • BOSTON • SYDNEY • AUCKLAND

First published in 2010
by Walker Books Australia Pty Ltd
Locked Bag 22, Newtown
NSW 2042 Australia
www.walkerbooks.com.au

National Library of Australia Cataloguing-in-Publication entry:
Branford, Anna.
Violet Mackerel's brilliant plot / Anna Branford; illustrator, Sarah Davis.
ISBN: 978 1 921529 17 7 (hbk.)
For primary school age.
Other Authors/Contributors: Davis, Sarah.
A823.4

The illustrations for this book were created with ink
and Derwent Inktense pencils
Violet's doodles designed by Zoe Davis
Violet's handwriting provided by Nikau Davis
Typeset in Bembo Regular
Printed and bound in China

10 9 8 7 6 5 4 3 2

THE
RED
BUTTON

Violet Mackerel is a girl with a theory.

Her theory is that when you are having a **very important** and brilliant idea, what generally happens is that you find something small and special on the ground. So whenever you spy a sequin, or a stray bead, or a bit of ribbon, or a button, you should always pick it up and try very hard to remember what you were thinking about at the precise moment when you spied it. Then think about that thing a lot more. That is Violet's theory, which she calls the

Theory of Finding

Small

Things.

"Wake up, Violet," says Violet's mum. "It's nearly five o'clock."

It is Saturday which is market day. Violet yawns. It is still dark. Mum's hair is a bit damp from her shower and it smells like mangoes and blossoms. Violet leans forward for a snuggle and nearly falls asleep again.

"Just stay awake until we're all in the van," says Mum. "Then you can sleep as much as you like."

Violet's big brother, Dylan, and big
sister, Nicola, are already awake and
they are helping to load up the van
with fold-up tables and chairs, the big
canopy umbrella, and boxes and baskets
of Mum's knitting. They are going to
the market like they do every Saturday
morning, to sell the woolly things Mum
makes.

Violet thinks she would quite like to wear her pyjama bottoms under her skirt today. They feel nice and warm from bed. Sometimes if you say things like "Can I wear my pyjama bottoms to the market?", people say things like "No." But if you just put your skirt on over the top, and have your eyebrows slightly raised like someone who is thinking of something **very important** and interesting, no one says anything at all.

When Violet, Mum, Nicola and Dylan arrive at the market, even though it is still not properly light, lots of people are already there, rugged up and rubbing their hands together with coldness, unfolding and unpacking their things to sell. No one notices Violet's pyjama bottoms.

Violet's favourite person at the market (apart from Mum and Dylan and Nicola and herself) is a man who never smiles. He sells china birds, small enough to fit in the palm of your hand, and he is there every week. Violet says hello to him as she always does, and he doesn't even look up, which he never does. But after waking up at nearly five o'clock in the morning, Violet doesn't feel much like chatting or smiling either. So she feels that even though he never says hello back, she and the man might share a sort of *understanding*.

The man's china birds are all different and all very dirty. Dylan says that they are probably brand-new from a factory. He thinks the man has just put dirt on them so they will look ancient and he can sell them for ten dollars instead of two. But Violet doubts it. She thinks it is much more likely that he is an archaeologist. She suspects that he specialises in digging up ancient china birds.

Violet would quite like to own one of the man's birds in particular. It is made of pale blue china, the colour of a robin's egg. It is always right at the back of the table.

And just as she is having that thought, out of the corner of her eye, Violet spies a small red button on the dusty market ground.

THE IMPORTANT IDEA

Violet picks up the red button.

She puts the button in her pyjama pocket, hidden by her skirt.
It is a safe and secret place.

"Right when I spied that red button," she says to herself, "I was thinking of how much I would like to own that BLUE CHINA BIRD. So now I know," thinks Violet, "that it was not just a silly wish but a **very important** idea."

However, the bird is ten dollars and Violet does not have ten dollars. Violet does not even have one dollar.

Violet thinks.

It is quite nice to hear the noisiness
and busyness of the market growing as
more and more people start to arrive,
but it can be a bit distracting when you are
trying to have a brilliant idea. So Violet
gets a blanket and a cushion out of the
back of the van and makes herself a sort
of nest in the back seat. From her nest,
Violet can still see what is going on at the
market, and she can think more clearly.

It is all right for Violet's sister, Nicola. She is a teenager and all she wants is a haircut by a person called Mojo who only works at a particular hair salon on Wednesdays.

Nicola has made earrings with wire and pliers. She is arranging them on the same table as Mum's woolly things. She is pinning them to a corkboard with a sign saying

Handmade earrings by
Nicola Mackerel $2

Violet likes Nicola's earrings and she thinks quite a few people will probably want to buy them.

It's also all right for her brother, Dylan. He is almost a teenager and all he wants is a camera. He is playing his violin next to Mum's stall with his violin case by his feet, and every few minutes Violet hears the jingle of people throwing coins into it.

Dylan only knows three songs, and one of them is a Christmas song, and it won't be Christmas for a very long time. But no one at the market seems to mind and he is getting quite a few coins to save for his camera.

When you only want something ordinary, like a camera or a haircut, you only need an ordinary plan, like playing the violin or making earrings. But if what you want is something **really, really important**, and if the importance has been proven by your **own personal theory**, then ordinary plans are no good.

What you need

is a *plot*.

A *brilliant* plot.

Fortunately, Mum keeps a notebook in the van and she doesn't mind people plotting in it. Violet reaches over to take the notebook and a pen out of the glove box and then rearranges her nest so she can rest the book on her knees. This is what she writes

Aim of plot =
To get the Blue China Bird

Actual plot =

beak
eye
(sun shaped) Patterns

Then it is just a matter of thinking
what
to
write
next.

THE THINKING SQUARE

Mum sometimes says that it is quite helpful, when you are trying to solve a difficult problem, to

outside the

think

square

Outside-the-square thinking is how Mum thought of doing knitting when Dad left and she was feeling sad. People made suggestions like

"Perhaps you could try jogging in the mornings."

and

"Why don't you take an evening class?"

But those are inside-the-square sorts of ideas, and not much good for people like Mum.

Knitting is different.

The blanket Violet is nesting in was
one of the first things Mum ever knitted.
She made it especially for Violet — soft
and feathery brown — because Violet likes
small brown sparrows, and she added
some purplish patches because actual
violets are purple. It is Violet's favourite
blanket.

Knitting makes Mum happy and
relaxed, even when the phone is ringing
and there is someone at the door,
and Dylan is yelling at Nicola, "IF
YOU DON'T GET OUT OF THE
BATHROOM NOW, I WILL TELL
ANGUS PODMORE THAT YOU
LOVE HIM," and Nicola is nearly crying
because she still has conditioner in her
hair and she *can't* come out. So Violet
thinks that knitting was quite a good idea
of Mum's.

Violet decides she might try the trick of thinking outside the square. So she crosses out the part in her notebook where she has written "**Actual plot**" and instead she draws a big thinking square. Inside the square she writes ordinary ideas, such as

a) tell Mum I need the Blue China Bird for a school project.
b) Ask for it for my birthday.

When the square is full of very ordinary ideas, she writes her interesting ideas outside it. These are things like

a) Dry ten corn kernels in the sun and paint them with white paint. Put them under the pillow and if the tooth fairy gets tricked and brings ten dollars, buy the Blue China Bird.

a) tell Mum I need the Blue China Bird for a school project.

b) Ask for it for my birthday.

Go on a TV game show where you win really big prizes like fridges, by guessing what the missing letters are in dr _ ss-ng- g- wn.

(Even though the clue is "something you wear over your pyjamas before bed and possibly also for a while in the morning ")

Then do a swap with the man for the Blue China Bird.

Violet likes these ideas, especially the ones outside the square, but she feels that she has not yet stumbled upon a **brilliant plot**. These are all only **quite good plots**.

Violet must have been thinking and plotting for a while and maybe even falling asleep a little bit (which is easy to do if you have made a very comfortable and warm nest), because Mum opens the van door and says, "Are you all right in there?"

"Yes," says Violet. "I'm just doing some plotting."

Violet decides to take a break from plotting because Mum has bought everyone some little pancakes called **poffertjes**. They come in a paper cup with a drizzle of maple syrup and a long pointy wooden skewer to spike them with. They are one of Violet's favourite things.

Violet sits by the knitting stall with Mum and Nicola and Dylan and they all spike at their poffertjes and get a bit sticky. And just as Violet is thinking about stickiness, and not actually about plotting at all, a funny thing happens. The beginning of a **brilliant plot** suddenly sprouts in her mind.

When she has finished her last poffertje, Violet crawls underneath the table of Mum's knitted things. She is hidden by the tablecloth hanging down so no one can see what she is doing. Using the pointy wooden skewer from her poffertjes, she begins to scratch in the dirt. The top layer crumbles easily away, so Violet digs some more, scooping the dirt into a little pile beside the growing hole with her hands.

"What are you doing?"
asks Mum after a while,
peeking under the
tablecloth.

"Being an **archaeologist**,"
says Violet.

A **good plot** is now settling properly
in Violet's mind. If she finds something
very precious, like an ancient jewel or
a rare dinosaur bone, she will become
rich and famous for her discovery. Then
she will be able to buy the BLUE CHINA BIRD.
It would be good to find even a very
small thing, just to be sure the idea is an
important one, but so far there is just
more dirt.

Violet scratches and scoops under the table. She doesn't find any ancient jewels or rare dinosaur bones. She takes the red button out of her hidden pyjama pocket and buries it in the dusty dirt. Finding things you have hidden yourself isn't quite as much fun as finding proper treasure, but it is much better than finding nothing.

Soon Mum is ready to pack up the stall and Nicola is saying that if she hears Dylan's Christmas carol one more time, she will chop off her own head.

Violet has not found any treasure. She hasn't even found anything ordinary, like a paperclip or a bottle top.

Just the red button, over and over again.

But she is not ready to give up just yet.

That afternoon when they get home, Violet's mum does her French lesson. She is learning from a set of CDs and a book.

"Red!" says the man on the CD.

"Roooooosh," says Mum.

"Green!" says the man on the CD.

"Vairrrrrr," says Mum, as if she has a hair in her mouth.

Mum has been trying lots of new things lately. Stuck to the wall in the kitchen is a small piece of paper on which she has written the words

If You Can See It, You Can Be It.

After Dad left, a few of these bits of paper started to appear around the house.

"Is that your theory?" Violet asks.

"Sort of," says Mum.

"What does it mean?" asks Violet.

"I think it means that if you can picture something very clearly in your *mind's eye*, you can make it happen."

Violet quite likes the idea that her mind has an eye.

"What does your *mind's eye* see?" Violet asks.

"Well, first, I see you and Dylan and Nicola growing up happy and healthy. And then when you are all grown up, I see myself in Paris, speaking French and maybe knitting scarves and leg warmers for a boutique or two," says Mum, squatting down to pick something up.

"What's that?" asks Violet.

"One of Nicola's earrings, I think," says Mum, putting it in her pocket, as Violet has explained the **Theory of Finding Small Things** to her before.

"If I am not *quite* grown up, can I come with you to Paris?" asks Violet.

"Yes," says Mum.

"And if I *am* properly grown up, I will send you postcards from my archaeological digs."

"I would like that," says Mum.

Violet goes to her room where she has taken her notebook of plots. At the top of the page she writes

If I Can See It, I Can Be It

Then she closes her eyes.

Her *mind's eye* sees all sorts of things, like herself on a talk show with the title

"Girl archaeologist discovers new dinosaur, to be named
Violetosaurus Mackerelus".

The talk show host says to her, "So, Violet, how did you actually find the bone that led to this incredible discovery?"

"Well, Max," says Violet (since Max seems to be the name her *mind's eye* has given to the talk show host), "there was a BLUE CHINA BIRD at the market, and I was thinking outside the square about how I could get it ..."

The studio audience says, "Ahhh!", because they think it is a nice sort of wish. But they are also amazed by her cleverness. They are all planning to send her china birds when they get home, so she will end up with hundreds of them. Probably all the talk show hosts will want to interview her after that. She might even be the richest and most famous dinosaur bone discoverer in the world.

Violet opens her eyes again. "**If I can see it, I can be it**," she says to herself.

Then she goes outside into the garden and the real dig begins.

THE ARCHAEOLOGICAL DIG

The wooden skewer from the markets was a good tool for digging under the table, but Violet suspects it is not the best tool for an **archaeologist**. There are proper spades and trowels in the garden shed which will make her job much easier. There are even some old, soft paintbrushes, perfect for getting the very last of the dirt off precious treasure or old bones. And there might be all kinds of interesting things buried in the garden. Violet hopes there will even be a stray sequin glittering in the grass in the sun, to show her exactly where to dig.

Violet assembles her **archaeologist's** toolkit and when it is complete, she scans the garden for a sparkling hint. But there is nothing. So she decides to start right in the middle, where the grass is nice and soft. It looks like just the sort of place a dinosaur bone might be.

Violet digs and digs and digs.
Sometimes she hits something hard
(which always turns out to be a rock or
a pipe, and not an ancient bone). Then
she works on making the holes wider
instead of deeper.

"If I can see it, I can be it," she says to herself.

As she digs, getting hotter and hotter and tireder and tireder, Violet makes sure she keeps on thinking about the *Violetosaurus Mackerelus*. It will probably get in the newspaper, maybe even on the front cover, as well as on Max's talk show. Then, when she is very rich and famous, Violet will buy Mum a whole rainbow of coloured wool. She will also buy Dylan a camera and Nicola a haircut by Mojo.

They will all say, "Violet, as well as being a brilliant plotter you are so generous, always thinking of other people and not of yourself."

(Although actually, first of all, she will buy herself the BLUE CHINA BIRD.)

Suddenly, Violet hears a sort of coughing, gasping noise.

She looks up.

It is Nicola, and she doesn't look as though she is thinking of Violet's generosity. In fact, she looks more as if Dylan has been talking to Angus Podmore.

"What ... are ... you ... *doing*?" she asks.

"I'm being an **archaeologist**," says Violet.

When she looks around her, though, she can see why Nicola's mouth is still a bit open. Their small back garden looks quite different with so much of the grass the wrong way up.

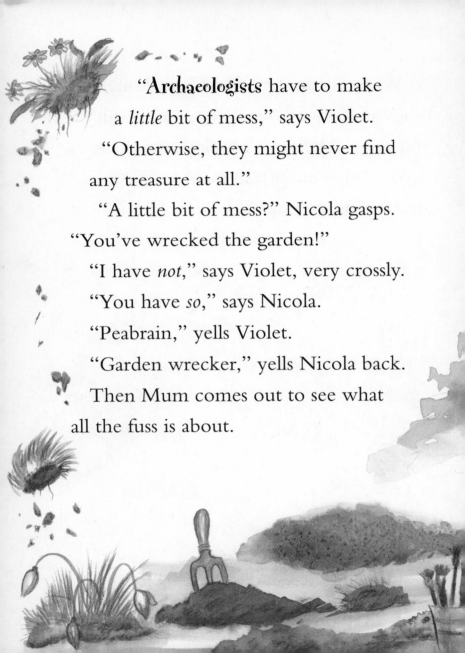

"**Archaeologists** have to make a *little* bit of mess," says Violet.

"Otherwise, they might never find any treasure at all."

"A little bit of mess?" Nicola gasps. "You've wrecked the garden!"

"I have *not*," says Violet, very crossly.

"You have *so*," says Nicola.

"Peabrain," yells Violet.

"Garden wrecker," yells Nicola back.

Then Mum comes out to see what all the fuss is about.

THE
SLIGHT
DISASTER

"**O**h, Violet," says Mum, putting both her hands over her mouth and then over her eyes. "What were you *thinking*?"

"I was thinking of a **brilliant plot**," says Violet in the crossest voice she has ever, ever used. Clearly, no one is being at *all* amazed by her generosity.

Somehow the discovery of *Violetosaurus Mackerelus*, the talk show and the newspaper, the rainbow of wool, the camera, the haircut by Mojo and even the BLUE CHINA BIRD seem to swirl and drain away like dirty bathwater.

Violet runs to her room and flops on the bed and howls and howls and her pillow gets wetter and wetter.

After a little while, Mum comes in and sits down on the bed next to her.

"Nicola said you were being an archaeologist again," says Mum.

"Yes," says Violet, into the pillow.

"There isn't any treasure in the back garden," says Mum.

"How do you know?" asks Violet, still into the pillow.

"Your dad and I shovelled that dirt there ourselves when we first bought the house, before you were born."

"Nobody ever tells me *anything*," says Violet, wondering what other important information they have all been keeping a secret.

"Maybe you could have asked before digging up the garden," says Mum.

Then there is more howling, followed by lots of hiccups and a difficult time talking.

Mum's hair still smells a bit like mangoes and blossoms. It is nice, when you are having a slight disaster, to smell something like that.

Violet says, "My *mind's eye* got it wrong."

"Mine sometimes does that too," says Mum.

"What do you do when your *mind's eye* gets it wrong?" asks Violet.

Mum thinks.

"Wait a bit and then try something different," she says.

Then Violet gets her notebook and she and Mum think outside the square together about the garden.

Mum looks out the window where the soft patch of grass was. She says she has always wanted a Japanese sort of garden, perhaps with a fish pond and lots of white pebbles. Violet quite likes the idea of a fish pond but she thinks white pebbles might not be very nice to lie on in the sunshine, which is one of the things she likes to do when the weather is warm.

Violet says she likes farm animals and has always rather wanted a farm, perhaps with some chickens, a sheep and a smallish cow, which would eat all the leftover grass so the holes would not be so noticeable. Mum says she quite likes farm animals too, but not necessarily in her own garden, since keeping a farm is a lot of work and also the neighbours might complain about all the clucking and mooing.

So in the end they decide to go to the plant nursery and buy a packet of bulbs, since the earth has been freshly turned and it is actually just the right time of year for planting them. Even though it is getting late by the time they get home, they neaten up the holes in the grass and plant the big, knobbly seeds in the soft, brown soil.

Violet is still disappointed, of course. It would have been much better to find some treasure or an ancient dinosaur bone, and to have been on a talk show, and best of all for the BLUE CHINA BIRD to be nesting on the table next to her bed. But even so, she quite likes thinking of daffodils and jonquils starting to grow where the treasure was supposed to be.

THE
LEG
WARMER

The next morning, Violet feels a bit better about the whole garden incident. Sunday mornings are a warm and peaceful time, since it is usually just Violet and Mum because Nicola has netball practice and Dylan has chess. Mum sits close to the heater and does knitting and Violet sits nearby, doing a puzzle.

"What's that going to be?" asks Violet, seeing the purple and blue wool weaving together like colours in a sunset.

"A bag," says Mum.

Violet watches Mum knitting. It doesn't look too hard.

The **archaeology** plot did not work out quite as brilliantly as she had hoped, but Violet has not forgotten the BLUE CHINA BIRD and her *mind's eye* is looking out for some new ideas. "Can I learn to knit?" asks Violet.

"Of course," says Mum, "when you're a bit older."

"I was thinking more like now," says Violet.

"Knitting is complicated," says Mum.

"I *like* complicated things," says Violet.

Mum has some knitting needles which are good for a beginner. While she is finding them, Violet does some more plotting in her notebook. The plotting is mostly a picture of some woolly cats and trousers and smallish trees and other things she might quite like to knit. Then maybe she could have her *own* stall at the market, right next to Mum's, and earn enough money to buy the BLUE CHINA BIRD. (Also, she might be the first person in the world ever to have actually knitted a small tree, so she might get to be on a talk show, after all).

Mum comes back with the needles and casts on some thick green wool for Violet.

"Now," says Mum. "You put the needle through, loop the wool around, bring the back needle forward, and flick the stitch off. Through, loop, forward and flick. Through, loop, forward and flick."

It turns out that two needles and a ball of thick green wool are a lot for two hands to manage, even before you start looping and flicking.

Mum fixes up the bit where most of the casting on got cast off.

"Have another try," says Mum.
"Through, loop, forward and flick."

Still it does not quite work.

Through, loop, re-loop and twist.

Through, doesn't look right, turn over and strange knot.

Try to undo, drop, forget which needle and get cross.

Mum does not have her look of Sunday morning peacefulness any more. She has more the look of when the toaster has made the smoke alarm go off and no one can find the car keys and Nicola is saying that she is the only person at her whole entire school who does not have a mobile phone.

"Knitting is a difficult thing to learn," says Mum. "That box is full of my mistakes."

Violet puts down the knitting needles and wool and looks in the box. Inside it are some woolly squares with slight holes in them, scarves which are not at all long enough, some socks which stop around the toes and one short wide tube with some big loose patches. It is made of lots of odds and ends of wool, all different colours, with spidery threads hanging from it. Violet quite likes the woolly tube, so she pulls it out of the box.

"What's this?" asks Violet.

"It was going to be a leg warmer," says Mum, but I dropped a stitch or two and anyway it is much too loose for a leg."

"Both my legs go in it easily." Violet tries it on. "With arms in too," she says.

"Exactly," says Mum.

Violet goes up to her room and brings down a box of threads and ribbons and buttons and sequins beads and other things she has spotted while having important ideas.

The first thing she chooses is a green sequin that fell off the sparkly cardigan Mum wore every day last winter. She pushes one of the loose ends of the leg warmer through the middle of the sequin and ties a knot in the end to hold it in place. Then she starts the job of threading something from her box onto every loose end, weaving the dangling threads backwards and forwards through the knitting until they almost disappear.

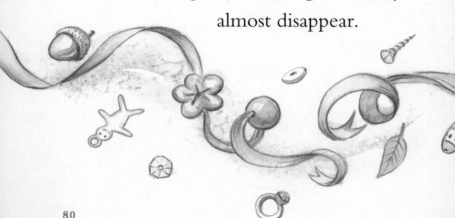

While she is sitting on the floor and working on the leg warmer, Violet spots under a chair one of the little gold links Nicola uses for her earrings.

Violet carefully weaves the small thing in with the other treasures.

Even though the leg warmer wasn't exactly part of her plot, perhaps it is part of an **important idea** anyway.

Every day after school that week, Violet works on the leg warmer. Slowly, it gains more colours and dangles, beads and bits and sparkles. On Friday, Violet threads on the red button she found at the market. It is a bit muddy from being buried and found so many times, but you can still see a lot of the redness. It is a very good final touch.

"Can I put it on the table at the market in the morning?" asks Violet.

"Yes." Mum smiles. "What will you call it?"

Violet thinks.

"It is called a *Tubular Scarf*," she says.

"It works like this."

She puts the leg warmer over her head and bunches it around her neck to show Mum. It fits loosely like a scarf.

"Plus you can do this," says Violet, pulling the back part over her head like a medieval hood.

Violet asks Mum for a shoebox to put the scarf in. But on the Friday night before the market, when the time has nearly come to put it inside and shut the lid, Violet finds that she would actually rather not.

If someone buys the *Tubular Scarf,* then maybe she will have enough money to buy the BLUE CHINA BIRD, which is **very important**. But Violet wonders if the person who buys it will know that it can be both a scarf and a hood. She wonders if they will notice all the small things woven into it, especially the red button. They might not realise that the scarf was made partly by her and partly by Mum. And all of those things are actually **quite important too**.

"Mum, do you ever secretly hope that people don't buy your knitted things, so you can keep them a bit longer?" Violet asks.

"Sometimes I decide I don't want anyone to buy them at all," says Mum, "so I keep them or give them to you or Nicola or Dylan."

"Giving things is different from keeping them *or* selling them," says Violet.

"Sometimes it's nicer," says Mum.

Nicola only needs to sell two pairs of earrings tomorrow and then she will have enough money to visit Mojo on Wednesday.

Dylan needs a bit more for his camera than he will probably get from playing his violin tomorrow, but he is still hopeful.

Violet suspects it is all quite easy
if what you want is something quite
ordinary, like a haircut or a camera. Then
you just do ordinary things, like making
earrings or playing the violin. But the
BLUE CHINA BIRD is a different *sort* of thing.
That is the problem.

Violet writes on the lid of the shoebox
with a purple marker.

Tubular Scarf made partly by

Violet Mackerel, $10

Then she puts the scarf in the box.
But for quite a long time she leaves the
lid off.

THE
SMILING
MAN

The next morning while it's still dark, Mum says, "Wake up, Violet. It's nearly five o'clock."

Violet decides she will wear her pyjama bottoms to the markets again, since last week she was especially nice and warm.

Nicola and Dylan help Mum carry things out to the van and Violet carries the box with the *Tubular Scarf*.

She keeps the box on her lap all the way to the market.

When they arrive Violet helps set up the stall.

"I'm not going to put the *Tubular Scarf* out just *yet*," she says to Mum. "First I think I will go for a small walk."

Violet walks over to the stall of the man who doesn't smile, so she can look at all the colours of the china birds on his table and check that the BLUE CHINA BIRD is there.

It is **not**.

The man is busy rummaging in his
van so Violet looks carefully at every
bird again, just to make
sure. Mum says it is
best not to worry until
you are quite sure there
is something to worry
about. But now Violet
has checked.

It is *definitely*
not there.

"Did somebody buy
the BLUE CHINA BIRD?" asks Violet, who has
a very uncomfortable feeling growing in
her chest.

The man does not turn around.

"DID SOMEBODY BUY THE **BLUE CHINA BIRD**?" Violet asks, much more loudly.

"Did you say something?" asks the man who doesn't smile.

And he smiles at Violet!

"Sorry, I am a bit deaf," he says.

"I asked you about the BLUE CHINA BIRD," says Violet, whose heart is bumping around inside her. "The one that is about the colour of a robin's egg."

"Oh, *that* one," he says. "I always unpack that bird last of all, because secretly I hope no one will buy it. It's my favourite."

The man takes the beautiful bird gently out of its scruffy newspaper packaging and puts it on the table. Gradually, Violet's chest goes back to normal.

"It's my favourite too," says Violet. "Did you find it on an **especially important** archaeological dig?"

"Pardon?" says the man.

"You are an **archaeologist**, aren't you?"

"No," says the man.

"What are you then?" asks Violet.

He thinks for a bit.

"A backpacker," he says. "I bought my china birds from a potter who I met when I was backpacking in Spain last year."

Violet thinks how nice grey eyes are with a green jumper, which is what the man has. But he looks as if he needs a jacket too. He is rubbing his hands together and blowing on them.

"You look cold," says Violet.

"Backpackers don't mind the cold too much," says the man, whose name turns out to be Vincent.

"The best thing for coldness," Violet tells him, "is to keep your pyjama bottoms on under your clothes. Hardly anyone notices."

"Really? I might try that next week," he says.

A thought is coming into Violet's mind. If smiling Vincent had a *Tubular Scarf*, he could be nice and warm *this* week.

And just as she is thinking it, she spies

a small stray piece of the coloured string Vincent uses to put paper tags on his birds. It has blown underneath the table.

Vincent says she can keep it, so Violet picks it up and puts it in her pocket.

Then she goes back to the van and gets out the shoebox with the scarf inside. She finds a pen in the glove box and scribbles out the part on the lid that says $10 but leaves on the part that says

Tubular Scarf made partly by

Violet Mackerel

She feels a bit shy going back.

"Hello again," says Vincent when he sees her. "What have you got there?"

"It's a *Tubular Scarf*," says Violet. "I partly made it."

"So I see," says Vincent, reading the box.

"Who made the rest?"

"My mum," says Violet.

"Is she the knitter a few stalls over?" asks Vincent.

"Yes," says Violet, "and she is also a learner of French."

"So am I," says Vincent. "In fact, I plan to go backpacking in France one day."

"Mum too," says Violet. "She sounds like she has a hair in her mouth."

"She *is* doing well then," says Vincent.

Violet opens the box and holds it out to Vincent. He takes the scarf out very carefully and tries it on. It fits him snugly and Violet thinks he looks warmer already. Then she shows him how you can also pull the back part up over your head like a medieval hood.

"What a good idea," says Vincent. "How much is it?"

"Nothing," says Violet. "It's a present."

Vincent smiles the nicest smile of all.

"I love it," he says. "I especially like the red button."

In a funny way, it is *almost* as good as having the BLUE CHINA BIRD, Violet thinks, to see him smiling and feeling warmer.

"Since your Mum partly made this,

do you think she would mind if I stopped by later on to say thank you?"

"I don't think she would mind," says Violet.

When Vincent does stop by a bit later, he is still wearing the *Tubular Scarf* and he puts quite a lot of money in Dylan's violin case.

"Christmas carols are my favourite," he says.

Mum smiles.

THE
BLUE CHINA
BIRD

Violet is still really only testing out the **Theory of Finding Small Things**. She is also realising that no **plot**, however **brilliant**, can be absolutely sure to work.

But on Monday, Dylan has enough money to buy his camera and now he is busy all the time — too busy, even, to say anything to anyone about Angus Podmore when Nicola is taking a very long time in the bathroom. He is always out in the garden, photographing the growing bulbs which have little green shoots already.

And on Wednesday afternoon, not only does Nicola go to see Mojo at the hair salon, but Mum goes too, and they both come home with coloured bits and straight bits and funny lengths at the back.

And that evening while Mum's hair is still special, Vincent comes round to eat a roast dinner and practise French. When he arrives he is wearing the *Tubular Scarf*, pulled up at the back like a medieval hood. They have to turn the volume up on the CD player as Vincent really is a bit deaf.

"Black!" says the man on the CD.

"Nwaaaaaar," says Mum.

"Nwaaaaaar," says Vincent, who now seems to smile all the time.

After dinner, while Mum and Nicola and Dylan are busy clearing away plates and putting sprinkles on ice-cream for dessert, Vincent takes something out of his pocket and gives it to Violet. It is wrapped in soft purple tissue paper.

"What is it?" asks Violet.

"A present," says Vincent.

Violet carefully unravels the purple tissue. Then, even more carefully, she unravels the scruffy newspaper underneath.

And after that, *Violet* smiles the nicest smile of all.

Because there in her hands, sitting in a soft nest of tissue and newspaper, is the BLUE CHINA BIRD.

How to make a Box of Small Things

If you would like to make a box of small things like Violet's, it is quite easy to do.

1. **The first thing you will need is a box.** The size and sort is up to you. An empty matchbox is handy because it will fit easily in your pocket, plus you can fit a surprising number of small things into a matchbox. A shoebox is also useful because you can fit even more small things in one of those. It all depends on what sorts of boxes are spare at your house.

2. The next thing is to make it very clear that this is not the sort of box that anyone should accidentally throw away, which you do by labelling it.

You could write something like

> ### Juliet's Box of Small Things

or

> ### Small Things Belonging to Lucy

or

> ### These Small Things are the Property of Thomas.

3. **The best boxes of small things tend to be decorated with drawings,** perhaps of the sorts of small things you plan to put inside.

4. **Then it is just a matter of searching for small things to put in your box.** You might have some you have been keeping already. People in your family might even have one or two that they don't mind giving you. But if not, you can always go for a walk and see what you can find.

These are some of the things you could look out for:

Beads, buttons, little bits of ribbon, paperclips, hair slides, small coins, sequins, pieces of lace, feathers, leaf skeletons, bits of confetti, stamps, coloured threads and strings, small pebbles (especially if they have an interesting shape), pieces of tumbled glass, charms, seashells, tiny crystals, seed pods, marbles and lost jigsaw puzzle pieces.

And don't forget, if you are lucky enough to spot one of these things when you are out walking, try to remember what you were thinking at the moment you spotted it. It might turn out to be

a **very**

important

idea.